For Jack and Jan.
M.B. & D.H.

For my lovely wife, Christine.
J. K.

Parent's Introduction

We Both Read is the first series of books designed to invite parents and children to share the reading of a story by taking turns reading aloud. This "shared reading" innovation, which was developed with reading education specialists, invites parents to read the more complex text and storyline on the left-hand pages. Then, children can be encouraged to read the right-hand pages, which feature less complex text and storyline, specifically written for the beginning reader.

Reading aloud is one of the most important activities parents can share with their child to assist them in their reading development. However, *We Both Read* goes beyond reading *to* a child and allows parents to share the reading *with* a child. *We Both Read* is so powerful and effective because it combines two key elements in learning: "modeling" (the parent reads) and "doing" (the child reads). The result is not only faster reading development for the child, but a much more enjoyable and enriching experience for both!

You may find it helpful to read the entire book aloud yourself the first time, then invite your child to participate in the second reading. In some books, a few more difficult words will first be introduced in the parent's text, distinguished with **bold lettering**. Pointing out, and even discussing, these words will help familiarize your child with them and help to build your child's vocabulary. Also, note that a "talking parent" icon ☺ precedes the parent's text and a "talking child" icon ☺ precedes the child's text.

We encourage you to share and interact with your child as you read the book together. If your child is having difficulty, you might want to mention a few things to help them. "Sounding out" is good, but it will not work with all words. Children can pick up clues about the words they are reading from the story, the context of the sentence, or even the pictures. Some stories have rhyming patterns that might help. It might also help them to touch the words with their finger as they read, to better connect the voice sound and the printed word.

Sharing the *We Both Read* books together will engage you and your child in an interactive adventure in reading! It is a fun and easy way to encourage and help your child to read—and a wonderful way to start them off on a lifetime of reading enjoyment!

We Both Read: Just Five More Minutes!

Text Copyright © 2008 by Marcy Brown and Dennis Haley
Illustrations Copyright © 2008 by Joe Kulka
All rights reserved

We Both Read® is a trademark of Treasure Bay, Inc.

Published by Treasure Bay, Inc.
40 Sir Francis Drake Boulevard
San Anselmo, CA 94960 USA

PRINTED IN SINGAPORE

Library of Congress Catalog Card Number: 2007932495

Hardcover ISBN-10: 1-60115-013-X
Hardcover ISBN-13: 978-1-60115-013-4
Paperback ISBN-10: 1-60115-014-8
Paperback ISBN-13: 978-1-60115-014-1

We Both Read® Books
Patent No. 5,957,693

Visit us online at:
www.webothread.com

WE BOTH READ®

Just Five More Minutes!

By Marcy Brown & Dennis Haley

Illustrations by Joe Kulka

TREASURE BAY

 "Mark! Bedtime!" It was my mom, telling me it was time for bed.

I wasn't tired at all, but Mom said it was getting late. I asked, "Could I please, please, PLEASE stay up a little longer? **Just five more minutes**?"

"Okay," said Mom.

 "Just five more minutes."

Then Mom said it would probably take me just five more minutes to do the things I had to do to get ready for bed!

She said I had to brush my teeth and **wash** my **face** and put my pajamas on. She said I better get started, so I went to the bathroom and brushed my teeth.

 I **washed** my **face.**

I took all of my pajamas out of my drawer and laid them out on my bed. It was going to take a really long **time** to decide which pair I should wear tonight.

 **"Time** is up," said Mom.

I couldn't believe it. How could five minutes be up already?

"Please, Mom," I said with a hopeful smile. "I'm still not tired, and I haven't said good night to my pets yet. Please, can I stay up a little longer?"

Mom frowned and asked, "How much longer?"

I said, . . .

...."Just five more minutes."

Mom agreed and I went right to work, saying good **night** to all of my pets.

I patted my dog, stroked my cat, hugged my hamster, kissed my turtle, and waved to my fish. Then I tucked Iguana Bob into his little bed and said, . . .

. . ."Good **night**, Bob."

🔊 I still had a few minutes left, so I hurried to the kitchen for a bedtime snack.

No ordinary snack would do. I made the **greatest** ice cream sundae in the whole wide world, with pineapple and pizza and a chocolate caramel cupcake!

It was **great!**

My extra five minutes were up, so I headed slowly back toward my bedroom. Then I spied the snowman I had built this afternoon, standing alone outside in the snow. He really needed a snowman friend!

Mom looked surprised when I told her. "You want to build another snowman now?" she asked. "How long will that take?"

I said, . . .

...."Just five more minutes."

"Well . . ." said Mom.

I knew she meant yes, so I raced out the door and got right to work. I made a whole family out of **snow** for my snowman.

I made a **snow** dog too.

Mom asked if I was finally ready for bed, and I told her that I would be ready **very** soon. All I had to do was finish the **neck** scarf I was making for my giraffe.

His **neck** gets **very** cold.

Mom asked how long it was going to take to make a scarf. I explained that my giraffe has a very long neck. Mom asked again, "How long will it take?"

I said, . . .

...."Just five more minutes."

 When the scarf was done, I climbed into bed. I still wasn't tired, but I closed my eyes.

My eyes popped open again as I remembered the dust bunnies under my bed. They just can't fall asleep until I **sing** them a lullaby!

They love it **when** I **sing**.

I would have gone right to sleep when the song was over, but a dinosaur showed up at my bedroom door. He asked me if I would tie his **shoes** and I told him, "No." I said, instead, I would teach him to tie them himself.

Now, he can tie his own **shoes**.

Mom thought it was very nice of me to be so helpful, but now it was time to go to bed. I said I would, but first I needed to deliver a letter to my pen-pal in China. "How long will that take?" Mom asked.

I said, . . .

...."Just five more minutes."

Mom really wanted me to go to sleep now, even though I wasn't tired at all. She helped me climb back into bed so she could tuck me in.

That's when I saw that no one had tucked the moon in for the night. *Someone* **would** have to take care of that, and that *someone* would have to be me.

I **would** be back soon!

Once the moon was safely tucked away for the night, I remembered there was one more stop I had to make before I could go to **sleep**.

I flew to Mount Rushmore to brush George Washington's teeth.

Now, he can go to **sleep** too!

On the way home I flew over Antarctica and saw some penguins playing volleyball. They asked if I'd like to play with them. It would have been impolite to say no, so I landed my ship and joined in their game.

"How long can you stay?" the penguins asked.

I said, . . .

..."Just five more minutes."

I was going straight home from there with no more stops. Then I looked down at the park and saw a **tiger** that needed my help. The tiger was stuck in a tree and it couldn't get down.

I had to help the **tiger**.

I finally made it back home and was on my way to bed when I heard the North **Wind** blowing loudly. I knew I couldn't possibly sleep with all that noise, so I politely asked if he could please blow more quietly.

The **wind** said he was sorry.

 At last, I climbed into my bed and Mom tucked me in. I still wasn't tired, but she said I had to go to sleep anyway.

I said I would try.

I did try and soon I was fast asleep. The next thing I knew, it was morning.

Mom came into my room and said, "Wake up, sleepyhead!"

I couldn't believe it was time to get up! I was so tired I couldn't even open my eyes, so I just groaned and said, "Please, Mom, . . .

 . . . just five more minutes!"

If you liked *Just Five More Minutes!*, here is another
We Both Read® Book you are sure to enjoy!

A very whimsical tale of a boy and his dog and their
fantastic dreamland adventures. This delightful tale
features fun and easy to read text for the very beginning
reader, such as "pigs that dig", "fish on a dish", and a
"dog on a frog." Both children and their parents will
love this We Both Read book!

To see all the We Both Read books that are available,
just go online to **www.webothread.com**